THE NILE FILES

Stories about Ancient Egypt

by Philip Wooderson

Illustrations by Andy Hammond

W
FRANKLIN WATTS

First published in 2000 by Franklin Watts
96 Leonard Street, London EC2A 4XD

Text © Philip Wooderson 2000
Illustrations © Andy Hammond 2000

Editor: Lesley Bilton
Designer: Jason Anscomb
Consultant: Dr Anne Millard, BA Hons, Dip Ed, PhD

A CIP catalogue record for this book
is available from the British Library

ISBN 0 7496 3652 1 (hbk)
     0 7496 3656 4 (pbk)

Dewey Classification 932

Printed in Great Britain

CONTENTS

1. THE VERY BEST OMENS?
In which Ptoni gains a tutor, and Ptiddles learns
how to count.

5

2. MEET THE LOCALS
In which the sphinx gets a chip on its shoulder,
and Dad meets Skribble.

9

3. DAD ACTS TOUGH
In which Dad and Ptoni visit the school for scribes,
and are introduced to some of the old boys.

15

4. VEGETABLE GARDEN?
In which Dad asks for his taxes, and Stupor meets
an old acquaintance.

23

5. BRIGHT STAR RICHES
In which the peasants tell their side of the story,
and Ptoni begins to guess the truth.

31

6. SCRIBES TELL LIES?
In which Blottumout gives a lecture, and the storm
gets closer.

41

7. STUPOR'S NOT STUPID
In which Ptoni reads some numbers, and Stupor
is finally understood.

49

8. HIRE-O-WHATSITS
In which Dad gets an idea, and the lads have to do
some work.

55

NILE FILE-O-FACTS

60

BY ORDER OF HIS HIGHNESS, PHARAOH
ARMENLEGUP

In thanks for services rendered, the bearer of
this royal scroll is granted the right to collect
all taxes (now overdue) on two farms – Strong
Bull Farm and Bright Star Farm, both owned by
the School for Scribes at Thickutt. Run by
Headmaster Blottumout.

Signed by

Chief Counsellor

DONUT

P.S. The fool who bears this is not a real Tax Collector,
because he's not trained as a scribe – so he can't read
this. Ha ha!

P.P.S. But don't take advantage. Or Pharaoh might get
peeved!

Dad was in a sunny mood, lounging in the stern of his boat, popping grapes into his mouth, as *Hefijuti* drifted down the Nile towards their destination – the school for scribes at Thickutt.

"Ah, this is the life. No more haggling. As Pharaoh's Tax Collector, I can claim ten per cent of everything they've got, lads. And they'll have to hand it over – or else."

A couple of the crew rubbed their hands. "Good for you, chief!"

"Should help you to pay our wages."

"And a little bit more would be generous, seeing as you're going to be so wealthy."

Dad was so convinced that he was going to get rich, he'd hired an old scribe to teach Ptoni how to read and write.* "So you'll grow up to be a scribe, and work for Pharaoh," Dad said. "It's the fast way to fame and fortune."

Ptoni wasn't so sure.

Stupor, the scribe, had lost all his teeth, so he lived off pots of beer. This not only made his words slurred, but fuddled his brain so much he kept drifting off to sleep.

"I'm not learning terribly fast, Dad."

Dad tilted his head. "Don't be so modest."

* You had to learn to write if you wanted a good job – see page 60

The only thing that Stupor had taught him was how to write a few numbers.

"For two potth of beer you do thith."

"For twenty potth, you do *thith*."

And Stupor had also told him you could read hieroglyphics either backwards or forwards, depending which way they were facing . . .

Dad grinned. "Keep your eyes open, Ptoni. and you might learn more at Blottumout's famous school. It's run for sons of the gentry, so there'll be lots of rich pickings."

Stupor opened one eye. "Bad omenth I thee before me."

Dad went a bit pale. "You said we'd do really well there."

"He means in the sky," said one of the lads, waving a hand at a dark cloud hanging over the desert. "We're due for a sand storm, I reckon, so it's lucky we're going ashore."

CHAPTER 2
MEET THE LOCALS

They had to share the small landing stage with another old trading boat. Two crewmen were struggling to unload a large stone sphinx in a crate, under the watchful eye of a clean little man in a white robe. He called to the lads, "Quick, quick! We need your help. This instant!"

"Excuse me?" The lads leant over the side. "Why don't *you* lend a hand?"

"I'm Skribble, Assistant Head Scribe at
Master Blottumout's School."

"Big deal. We're working for Pharaoh."

"On that clapped-out old tub?" sneered the
scribe, flashing his sharp ratty teeth.

"I won't have you mocking my boat. I'm a
Tax Collector," said Dad.

"You couldn't *spell* Tax Collector."

Dad's ears turned brilliant purple. "Stupor,"
he cried, "spell Tax Collector."

No one replied.

"Never mind," Dad carried on, "where's
my Royal Scroll?"

The old scribe had gone back to sleep, but
Ptoni managed to find the scroll underneath

some old bedding clothes. Dad hastily unrolled
it to show off Pharaoh's seal.

Skribble took a step backwards.

"That's a very fine sphinx," said Dad,
enjoying Skribble's confusion. "If you had ten
of those sphinxes, I could take one for myself."

"Where would we put it?" asked Ptoni.

"We'd need a nice villa," said Dad. "Then
it could stand by the front door and –"

"Aaaaaargh!"

CRASH!

The crewmen had been struggling to heave the sphinx out of the boat, but now it was upside down, with a bad chip on its shoulder.

"If it's too heavy," Dad offered, "I could lend you my lads in return for –"

"Dad!" Ptoni gave him a nudge.

But Skribble was now all smiles. "That silly sphinx isn't for us, sire. My goodness, we couldn't afford it. It was ordered by one of our wealthier neighbours. But may I ask what brings *you* here?"

"Your taxes, of course."

Skribble flexed his thin lips. "But the Tax Collector has been here, sire. You can't mean we have to pay twice?"

Dad flapped the scroll. "It's all down here. There's tax overdue on two farms."

Skribble sucked in his cheeks. "These two little farms had nothing to pay, so nothing can

be overdue. And we're rather busy today. We have an important guest – the High Priest from the Temple of Amun. But you can come up to the school to read through our scrolls, if you want to."

Dad looked a bit worried about this. "We'd better bring Stupor, Ptoni."

CHAPTER 3
DAD ACTS TOUGH

With Stupor wheezing behind them, Skribble led Dad and Ptoni up the dusty track, through orchards laden with fruit.

"Good harvest!" said Dad.

"Not so far," snapped Skribble.

Dad winked at Ptoni. "He's worried. Let's stay till the harvest is gathered. I bet they've got comfortable guest rooms."

"Localth!" said Stupor. "Can't stand 'em."

"What locals?"

"He must mean the boys," sniffed Skribble, as they went through the gateway. "But no local boys are allowed here. We only take the sons of the gentry. They spend their days studying scribeship."*

"Just like *my* son," said Dad.

Skribble looked slightly more hopeful. "Why don't you enrol the boy. We could give a slight discount on fees if –"

"No thanks," put in Ptoni quickly.

"My boy has his own private tutor." Dad

* You had to study for a long time – see page 61

unrolled his scroll. "Now, let's get down to business!"

Skribble skimmed a few lines, reading the last bit quite closely. He looked up and grinned. "Yes indeed. It all seems quite clear to me now. There's been a small clerical error. Some junior scribe at the palace has sent you on a fool's errand."

Dad gawped at him. "How do you mean?"

Skribble handed the scroll back. "My dear chap, before we go any further, I think I should show you something."

Leading them into the school house, he pointed at some large panels lining the walls.

"On this one, you'll see the Roll of Honour of our most illustrious pupils. At the top – Grubbiflub – now Chief Inspector of Taxes. He keeps a fond eye on his old school, and comes down very hard on any *minor* officials who think they can turn up here and stir up mischief. You'd be very silly to cross him."

Dad seemed to think for a moment. "You know, I had lunch with him once, at Merchant Kashpot's place. But he's just a *minor* official, like me, compared to the person who signed this scroll – Pharaoh's Chief Counsellor, Donut. *You'd* be very silly to cross *HIM*!"

Skribble sucked in his cheeks.

"So there!" Dad rubbed his hands. "What's on those other panels?"

Skribble shot a sharp glance at Dad. "I'm sure you can read them yourself."

"I've got a slight headache," said Dad. "Er . . . Stupor?"

Stupor lowered his beer pot.

"Forget it," Skribble said crossly. "They just list the school's main assets. A papyrus plantation and workshops to make our own scrolls.* And I have a little sideline printing the finer details onto the mummy caskets at the shrine of Anubis. But Grubbiflub taxed us

---

* Papyrus was made from reeds – see page 62

fairly, after taking into account the high
running costs of this school."

"But not the two farms, though," Dad
reminded him. "Aren't they marked on your
panels?"

"Of course, yes – the one in the middle –
but I told you, you're wasting your time. I
mean they grow nothing at all."

"Nothing?" said Dad, with an innocent
grin. "What sort of farmer grows nothing?"

"I'm a scribe, not a stupid peasant. How
should I know?"

"Fine," said Dad. "In that case, why don't I see for myself?"

"That's sorted *him* out," said Dad as they trudged back down the track, passing a couple of peasants picking fat bunches of grapes and putting them into big baskets. "One in ten of those baskets will soon be ours. I'm good at this, aren't I Ptoni?"

Ptoni said nothing.

Skribble had given them directions to reach the larger farm. He'd said that they should follow the posts marked with a star, turning right when they got to the fork.

"Here's the fork, Dad. You've gone right past it."

"I've got a hunch we should go left."

"But Skribble said –"

"Skribble doesn't want us to collect any taxes. Look at that great big farmhouse!"

It certainly did look smart, with pillars, palm trees, and gardens with shady bowers and statues.

"Looks like Kashpot's palace," said Dad, wiping the dust from his knees. "I could do with a mobile throne for this. First impressions count a lot when you're tax collecting. Try and act like my servants, you two."

As they approached the grand entrance, a servant girl popped her head round the doorway.

Dad said, "I'm from Chief Counsellor Donut, to take Pharaoh's dues. Fetch your master."

The girl called up the stairs. "There's some sort of dirty trader outside saying he's come from Pharaoh."

A fat man, who looked like an old bull, appeared at the top of the stairs. "Not today thank you, I'm busy."

"Taxes," Dad cried.

"What about them?"

Dad unrolled the scroll. "Read it, Stupor."

The old scribe squinted at it.

"Out loud!"

Stupor rubbed his eyes, and taking the scroll from Dad, held it an inch from his nose.

The fat man guffawed. "I know Stupor. He taught at my old school – until I fired him!"

Stupor looked up and blinked. "Oh no, Blottumout!"

"Still pretending you know how to read?"

"But *you* can't have fired him," said Dad.

"I happen to be the Master of this School for Scribes."

"So you're not a farmer?"

"A farmer? You think I'd get my hands dirty?"

"But this is your farm?" asked Ptoni.

"This is a place of retreat. For contemplation and study."

"So who grows the grapes?" Dad burbled.

"How should I know? Why should I care? We just have a vegetable garden, providing the fare for our table."

"Well, I shall want proof," Dad insisted.

"Not now," said Blottumout firmly.

"But I'm a Tax Collector."

Blottumout curled his lip. "And I have the Lord High Priest from the Temple of Amun coming for lunch."

"I answer only to Pharaoh. And to Donut as well," said Dad.

Blottumout wavered slightly. "Perhaps you'd like to come in and have lunch then? We have some fried fish and roast ducks."

Dad looked a bit undecided. "Tax collecting is hungry work."

"And thirthtee doo," added Stupor.

"Palm wine," said Blottumout, taking down a pot and pouring wine into three goblets. "And maybe you'd do me the honour of reading the text for the lecture I'm giving this afternoon. You could give us your views while we eat?"

Dad didn't look quite so hungry. He glanced round. "Storm's on the way . . ."

Stupor drained Dad's goblet of wine. "And a playth of localth!"

"Shut up. We don't want to hear about locals."

Blottumout smiled. "Yes you will. Stupor must be referring to the other farm. It's much bigger than this and it's run by two crafty locals."

Stupor knocked back his third goblet and Blottumout quickly refilled it. "Follow the signs for the Bright Star Farm – but don't let them fool you, my friends. Don't listen, show them no mercy, and sting 'em for all they've got."

CHAPTER 5
BRIGHT STAR RICHES

Walking back to the fork in the track, Ptoni noticed that the peasants had gone, leaving their baskets of grapes.

"Thouldn't be left. Locals gettum," Stupor said to himself.

"Then we'll get 'em back," said Dad. "If Blottumout's place was the small farm, just think what the big one will be like. We'll get them to give us a slap-up lunch without any chat about lectures – then take what we want from their barns. That's Tax Collecting. I love it."

Ptoni wasn't so sure.

As they trudged round the next corner, he saw a big stone object dumped upside down in a ditch.

Dad wanted a closer look. He sank up to his knees in the water. But he didn't care. "It's the sphinx – the one we saw being unloaded."

REDUCED

MADE IN EGYPT

"But why have they dumped it?" asked Ptoni.

Dad had a wild grin on his face. "Skribble was telling us the truth. Some wealthy neighbours *have* bought it – the locals at Bright Star Farm. They must have tried to hide it when they heard I was coming. Now let them try and pretend they're not rich!"

But when they got round the next bend, instead of the big swanky palace Dad was expecting to find, there was only a run-down shack.

Dad entered the dusty yard, sending two skinny geese squawking off into the bushes.

"This must be the labourers' quarters."

Lifting a sheet of stained linen, he ducked his head through the low doorway. "You peasants!" he said. "Where's the villa?"

A thin little man and his wife were squatting on the mud floor. Ptoni had seen them before. They had been picking the grapes.

"What villa?" said the wife, blankly.

"Blottumout's villa? You ought to have taken the left fork."

"We did," Dad said. "Blottumout told us that Bright Star Farm was much bigger."

"So why do we have to work on *his* land to save ourselves from starving?"

"I happen to know," said Dad, "that he's only got a vegetable garden."

"It's a very big vegetable garden."

Dad refused to be daunted. "I am entitled to take one tenth of all your produce."

"And very welcome," the woman replied. "One tenth of nothing – what's that worth?"

"Nothing?" Dad echoed.

"Afraid so."

"So what do you live on?" asked Ptoni.

The poor peasants glanced at each other.

"That's got 'em," said Dad. "What's for lunch?"

"Boiled papyrus root," said the woman. "It's in the pot on the fire."

Dad gave them a twisted grin. "I warn you, I come from Pharaoh."

"So did your colleague," she said.

"Grubbiflub," said her husband. "We were doing all right until he came and stayed in Blottumout's villa."

"What's that got to do with my lunch?"

The thin little man gave a sigh. "He wouldn't believe that we only produced enough to feed ourselves – so he took the whole lot, and our tools too."

"But how could he do that," said Ptoni. "He ought to have left you nine-tenths."

"We begged Blottumout to help us, but he said that Grubbiflub must

have worked it out because he'd consulted the panels up on the schoolhouse wall. They've been there for hundreds of years."

"That's right." Dad was nodding his head. "Those panels can't lie – so *you're* lying. If you were as poor as you claim you are, you wouldn't have bought a posh sphinx."

"We never –"

"What sphinx, your Scribeship?"

"I think they're telling the truth, Dad."

Dad looked at Ptoni in horror.

Ptoni tried to explain. "Blottumout's got the big farm. But because Grubbiflub was his former pupil, he gets away with pretending

he's just got a vegetable garden. So the school doesn't have to pay any taxes. I bet you he bought the sphinx too. His garden's crowded with statues."

"Why was the sphinx brought here then?"

Ptoni tried to stay patient. "To hide it from us, of course."

Dad sighed. "So what do we do?"

Ptoni turned back to the thin man. "Have you checked what it says about this farm on the panels in the schoolhouse?"

"How could we do that? We can't read."

The woman grabbed Dad by the elbow. "Perhaps if you'd have a look, sire?"

Dad looked a bit uneasy. "I suppose I could ask my scribe here." He turned, but

Stupor was outside, slumped in the dusty yard with an empty pot in his lap.

"He might need a hand," said the woman.

Stupor needed more than a hand. He had to be pushed and pulled. And halfway up the track, he turned to look back at the river. It was almost invisible now, hidden in the shadows cast by a dense dark cloud. He mumbled again. "Localth coming. Won't get any taxeth when those localth awive."

"He's mad. Ignore him," said Dad.

The schoolhouse was quiet now. There

wasn't a boy to be seen. "I don't suppose sons of gentry have afternoon lessons," said Dad, "so we can look at those panels without being spotted. That's good."

He flung open the door.

"No, it isn't."

The room was packed with boys, squatting on the floor, facing a long low platform where a frail old High Priest was stretched out on a couch, listening to Blottumout's lecture.

Blottumout stopped in mid sentence. The boys all looked round.

"Sorry," Dad said.

Blottumout beamed. "Please join us. A Tax Collector, dear boys. A shining example of what you can become if you work hard at your studies."

The boys all smirked and tittered.

Dad's legs were still splattered with mud from scrambling into the ditch. His scroll was

covered with mud too. And Stupor was just behind him, eyes shut and mouth wide open, propped up by the two poor peasants.

"To what do we owe this great pleasure?"

Dad waved a hand at the panels up above Blottumout's head. "Just need to check up on a small point."

"Indeed, reading is so important. It is sometimes necessary to check on small points. You hear that, boys?"

Dad stared at the painted panels.

"But tell us, please, why it's important."

"Important," Dad gabbled. "I'll tell you. So you won't get fooled by people – people who know how to write!"

"Only scribes can write," said the frail old priest. "And scribes are all honourable men. Why should they fool anybody?"

"Someone's fooled these poor farmers," said Ptoni.

"They're ignorant peasants," scoffed Blottumout.

"That's why they rely on scribes," said the frail priest, very calmly. "Scribes never tell lies, do they Skribble?"

"Oh certainly not. No, Your Worship."

"Our word is the Truth," agreed Blottumout, turning to gaze at the panels. "Feel free to read everything up there."

"Stupor," hissed Dad.

The farmer's wife gave Stupor a dig in the ribs. He grunted, then went back to snoring.

Dad looked even more desperate. "Ptoni?"

"I'm just starting to learn, Dad."

"We will be patient," said Blottumout.

Ptoni stared at the central panel. It only had a few lines of script. The symbols on the first line included one that looked like a bull. The one below showed a star. "It names the two farms."

"Most impressive." Blottumout turned to the boys. "Now can one of you tell me which

of the farms has the most land?"

Ptoni remembered Stupor showing him how to do numbers.

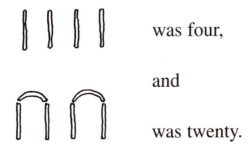 was four,

and

was twenty.

"The Bright Star Farm," they all shouted. "It's got twenty plots. It's enormous."

The poor farmers lowered their heads.

"What about Strong Bull Farm?"

"It's only got four!"

"So which farm must pay the most taxes?"

"The Bright Star Farm," they all chorused.

"Well done, boys," Blottumout beamed. "That's how the great Grubbiflub knew those two miserable peasants were farming so much land they were trying to hide their produce – because he could read hieroglyphics."

"But we've seen their farm," cried Ptoni. "They've only got two skinny geese, and four parched fields."

"Serves them right too." The High Priest wiped his hands. "Dishonesty has to be punished."

"But we never meant –" said the farmer's wife.

"Oh, quiet," said the farmer. "It's fate."

CHAPTER 7
STUPOR'S NOT STUPID

So that was that, thought Ptoni. Except that, looking up at the central panel again, he couldn't help wondering why some of the paint on those numbers looked so bright and new, and other bits looked faded and old.

"Excuse me."

"Yes," beamed Blottumout.

"Who repainted those numbers for Bright Star Farm?"

"How should I know? Some piddling junior scribe –" He turned to Skribble. "You did it."

Skribble shrank into his couch.

"What does it matter?" the priest asked.

"He made a mistake," said Ptoni.

"I don't make mistakes," cried Skribble. "I did it like Blottumout told me."

"And why would –?" Dad scratched his head. "I mean, it can't make any difference."

"It does," said Ptoni. "Can't you see – he added on new bits at the top, joining up those old uprights. That's why it looks as if Bright Star Farm has twenty plots of land."

"But if he'd done that," said the High Priest, "both farms would be down for twenty!"

Ptoni stared at the panel again. The High Priest was right, of course, except . . . the four bold uprights marked for Strong Bull Farm did have very faint lines joining each pair of uprights, as if . . .

"Excuse me, Your Worship. Those top lines have been painted out."

"Whatever for?" gasped the priest.

"Why do you think," Dad broke in, giving Ptoni a thump on the back. "To wangle Blottumout's villa out of paying its rightful taxes!"

Blottumout's chins started wobbling.

The High Priest struggled to sit up. "Blottumout. Quickly. Deny it!"

"I s-s-swear on my honour," he stuttered, "if I tell a lie may the gods –"

"Play some locals," said Stupor.

"Sounds reasonable," said the High Priest, raising his stick in the air. "If Blottumout lies, the god Amun will show his great displeasure by sending PLAGUES OF LOCUSTS!"*

Ptoni and Dad swopped glances.

"Is that what you meant?" Dad asked Stupor.

"What did youth ink I meant? I bin twying to tell you all day!"

They all rushed out to the courtyard.

* Locusts could do lots of damage – see page 63

The sky was black overhead. But instead of great gusts of sand, nasty black twitching things were tumbling through the air, bouncing off the ground, making a loud buzzing noise.

CHAPTER 8
HIRE-O-WHATSITS

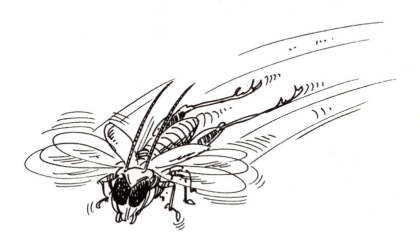

"They'll ruin the grapes," yelled the farmer's wife.

"We'll have lost the whole crop," cried the farmer.

"It's Blottumout's loss," said Dad.

"But ten per cent would have been ours, Dad."

Dad's smile disappeared. "Not just ten per cent," he said faintly. "Blottumout tried to cheat us – and that means he tried to cheat Pharaoh – and that means he ought to be punished." His eyes went wide and glassy. "So we could claim THE WHOLE LOT!"

"The locusts have claimed the whole lot, Dad."

"So what can we take instead?"

"Phinkth," said Stupor flatly.

"Of course we're both thinking," screamed Dad.

"Not phinking. Thwinkth!" Stupor told them.

"He means that stone sphinx," said Ptoni.

Dad swotted a big black locust off the tip of Stupor's nose. "Do you think the lads could move it?"

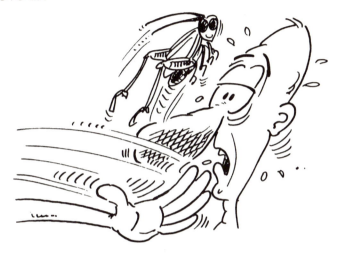

"They haven't done anything else today."

"Need help from the locuth!" said Stupor.

"Help from the locals?" said Ptoni.

But Dad didn't hear. "Help from the locusts? They got us into this mess! But on the other hand," Dad sighed, "we'd be in a far worse mess if I hadn't had the foresight to hire a private tutor for you, to teach you those squiggly whatsits."

"Hieroglyphs," murmured Ptoni.

"Wasted on scribes," Dad said sagely. "But don't you go scorning them, Ptoni. I think these hire-o-whatsits might turn out quite helpful for trading. We might even hire that sphinx out. For private parties."

"Thtupid!" Stupor drew himself upright. "The dwinkth will be jinkthed. I warn oo. Learning to weed ith more helpful."

Dad stared at him. "Weed? Weed what?"

Ptoni took a deep breath. "He means *read*, Dad. Like I read those Helpful Hieroglyphs!"

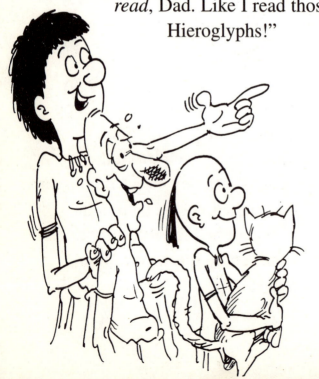

Hieroglyphics

Egyptians used a complicated writing system
known as hieroglyphics. There were more than
700 different symbols to learn, and there were
many different ways of writing them.
Hieroglyphs could be written from left to right,
right to left, or top to bottom. Very few
Egyptians learnt to read and write. They relied
on scribes to do it for them.

Schools for scribes

A scribe was often the son of a scribe and was taught to write by his father. But as more and more scribes were needed, special schools were set up to train them. It took four or five years for them to master hieroglyphics, but once they did, they were guaranteed a good job for life!

Papyrus

Egyptians wrote on a paper-like material called papyrus. It was made by taking the pith from riverside reeds and pounding it into smooth sheets. The papyrus was then polished, to give a smooth flat surface. To make a book, several sheets were fixed together to form a scroll, which the scribe unwound with his left hand as he wrote.

Schoolboys wrote their exercises on wooden tablets or broken bits of pottery. These materials were much cheaper than papyrus.

Locusts

Locusts are very large grasshoppers. They breed quickly and, when vegetation and weather conditions are suitable, they can form swarms of up to 50 billion locusts. These swarms can devastate entire crops, eating everything that grows, and bringing famine.

Join Ptoni and his Dad up the Nile
in these other books.

THE SCRUNCHY SCARAB

07496 3649 1 (Hbk)   07496 3653 X (Pbk)

The town of Feruka is having a big celebration, but all Dad
has to sell are some dried-up figs and a few old flasks of oil.
Fortunately Ptoni finds a lucky scarab beetle – so perhaps
things will change for the better?

THE MISSING MUMMY

07496 3650 5 (Hbk)   07496 3654 8 (Pbk)

Dad goes to collect some wine he is owed by Slosh, the
merchant. But poor Slosh has died, and someone has stolen
his mummy. It's up to Ptoni to find it, and to claim the wine.

THE FEARFUL PHARAOH

07496 3651 3 (Hbk)   07496 3655 6 (Pbk)

Pharaoh Armenlegup is having a big festival to celebrate his
long reign. So everybody is happy – everybody, that is,
except Dad. He's been sentenced to death!